The Adventures of Inspector Eduardo:
The Nut Case

by Eleanor Weeks

Eleanor Weeks

DORRANCE
PUBLISHING CO
EST. 1920
PITTSBURGH, PENNSYLVANIA 15238

Dorrance Publishing Co
585 Alpha Drive
Suite 103
Pittsburgh, PA 15238
Visit our website at *www.dorrancebookstore.com*

ISBN: 978-1-4809-1871-9
eISBN: 978-1-4809-1848-1

Cast of Characters

Inspector Eduardo: A gecko with a mustache wearing horn-rimmed glasses and a cap.

Mr. Busco: A bear in a black vest with gold buttons.

Store Clerk: A white poodle in a blue striped dress.

Laddy Hippo: A hippo in a red and white polka dot dress.

Squirrel: A squirrel dressed in a blue and white pinstripe suit.

Constable Henry: A Great Dane in a brown uniform and a Mountie-like hat.

Statue of Mayor Rocky: A raccoon in a brown and white stripped jacket.

The Adventures of Inspector Eduardo:
The Nut Case

"Hey inspector come quickly. Someone broke into the country store last night and made an awful mess. The thief ransacked the place, knocking over barrels of apples, potatoes, and onions. The funny thing is that the register was not touched. The money is still there. Who could have done this?"

Mr. Busco, the owner of the store, could not find anything missing except three sacks of red pistachio nuts.

Inspector Eduardo began questioning the clerk who worked in the store. He asked Mrs. Pepper if she saw anyone suspicious looking in the store yesterday.

She said, "Everyone who came in was a regular, except two people. One was a pretty lady dressed in a black and white polka dot dress, and the other a man in a blue pin stripes."

Inspector Eduardo decided to check out the park across the street from the store. He met up with Constable Henry, who was patrolling near the water fountain. They stood there talking a while and the inspector looked in the water and saw nutshells at the bottom of the pool.

The inspector asked Constable Henry, "Have you seen anyone eating nuts by the pool?"

He said, "No!"

Inspector Eduardo told him to keep an eye out for anyone who might look suspicious.

The inspector was getting into his car when he looked down and saw red nutshells on the ground. He decided to follow the trail of shells, which led him into the park toward the big statue of Mayor Rocky.

The trail of nuts stopped at the foot of the statue. He looked around and did not see anyone. He started to walk away when he heard what he thought was someone sneezing. He decided to climb up on the rocks to get a better look at the statue. When he looked at the mayor's face, he saw his mouth was outlined in red. Just then, the statue sneezed and Inspector Eduardo fell backwards into the pool.

Rocky jumped off the pedestal and started to run away, but the inspector climbed out of the pool, grabbed him, and knocked him down. He handcuffed him and took him to jail.

Everyone heard about it the next day. They all came to the jail to congratulate Inspector Eduardo on a job well done.

It was all in a day's work for the inspector.